Fluent Reader titles are ideal for children who can confidently read books with a wider vocabulary, and who are beginning to read longer stories by themselves.

Special features:

.... Full, exciting story

.... Richer, more varied vocabulary

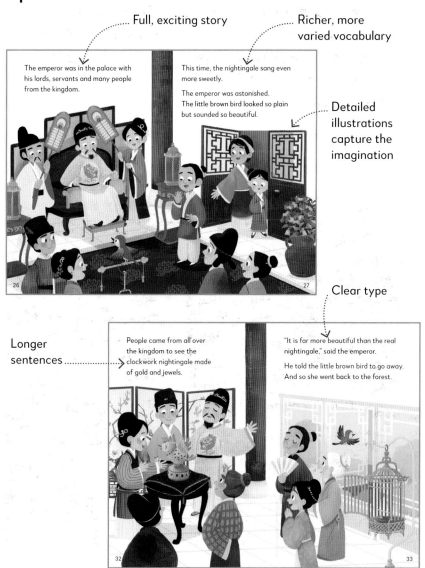

The emperor was in the palace with his lords, servants and many people from the kingdom.

This time, the nightingale sang even more sweetly.

The emperor was astonished. The little brown bird looked so plain but sounded so beautiful.

.... Detailed illustrations capture the imagination

26

27

.... Clear type

Longer sentences ....>

People came from all over the kingdom to see the clockwork nightingale made of gold and jewels.

"It is far more beautiful than the real nightingale," said the emperor.

He told the little brown bird to go away. And so she went back to the forest.

32

33

Ladybird

Education Consultant: James Clements
Book Banding Consultant: Kate Ruttle

LADYBIRD BOOKS

UK | USA | Canada | Ireland | Australia
India | New Zealand | South Africa

Ladybird Books is part of the Penguin Random House group of companies
whose addresses can be found at global.penguinrandomhouse.com.

www.penguin.co.uk   www.puffin.co.uk   www.ladybird.co.uk

First published 2024
001

Text adapted by Helen Mortimer
Text copyright © Ladybird Books Ltd, 2024
Illustrations by Leesh Li
Illustrations copyright © Ladybird Books Ltd, 2024

The moral right of the illustrator has been asserted

Printed in China

The authorized representative in the EEA is Penguin Random House Ireland,
Morrison Chambers, 32 Nassau Street, Dublin D02 YH68

A CIP catalogue record for this book is available from the British Library

ISBN: 978-0-241-56380-9

All correspondence to:
Ladybird Books
Penguin Random House Children's
One Embassy Gardens, 8 Viaduct Gardens, London SW11 7BW

MIX
Paper from
responsible sources
FSC
www.fsc.org   FSC® C018179

The Emperor
and the
Nightingale

Adapted by Helen Mortimer
Illustrated by Leesh Li

Many years ago in China, there lived an emperor.

He lived in a big, beautiful palace made of porcelain.

All around the palace was a beautiful
garden. It was so big that no one knew
how far it went. Even the gardener
did not know.

All around the garden was a big, beautiful forest.

A little nightingale lived in the forest.
People loved to listen to the nightingale.
"How sweetly she sings!" they said.

Many people came to China to see the emperor's kingdom.

Some wrote books about how much they loved the porcelain palace. Some wrote about how much they loved the beautiful garden. But the people loved the nightingale best of all.

The emperor read the books.
One day, he read about the nightingale.

"I'm the emperor! How do I not know
of this little bird?" he thought.

13

At once, the emperor called for one of his lords.

"I have read about the nightingale," he said. "Find her for me! I want to listen to her sing."

First, the lord asked everyone in the palace. But no one knew of the little bird.

The lord went outside and asked the gardener to help him look for the nightingale in the garden. But they could not find it.

A little girl was in the garden.
"I can help you find the nightingale,"
she said. "She lives in the forest."

So, the lord went with the little girl.

First, they saw a cow.

"Moo! Moo!" said the cow.

"Oh! Is that the nightingale?"
cried the lord.

The little girl shook her head and laughed. "No, my lord, that is a cow!" she said.

Then, they saw a frog.

"Ribbit! Ribbit!" said the frog.

"Oh! Is that the nightingale?"
cried the lord.

The little girl shook her head and laughed. "No, my lord, that is a frog!" she said.

They came to the forest.

And then, suddenly, the
nightingale sang.

"THAT is the nightingale,"
said the little girl.

22

The lord was astonished.
The little brown bird looked so plain
but sounded so beautiful.

"Will you come to the palace and sing for the emperor?" the lord asked the nightingale.

"My song sounds best in the forest," said the nightingale. "But I will come to please the emperor."

So, they all went back to the palace.

The emperor was in the palace with his lords, servants and many people from the kingdom.

This time, the nightingale sang even more sweetly.

The emperor was astonished.
The little brown bird looked so plain but sounded so beautiful.

From then on, the nightingale was kept in a gold cage. She even had her own servants.

People came from all over the kingdom to listen to her sing.

One day, a box came for the emperor.
In the box was a beautiful clockwork
nightingale made of gold and jewels.

It could sing as sweetly as the real nightingale in her cage. But it had just one song that it sang over and over.

People came from all over the kingdom to see the clockwork nightingale made of gold and jewels.

"It is far more beautiful than the real nightingale," said the emperor.

He told the little brown bird to go away. And so she went back to the forest.

The emperor kept the clockwork
nightingale next to his bed.
It sang for him every day.

A year passed. Then one night,
the clockwork nightingale would
not sing.

It was broken! The emperor called for his lords to fix it, but no one could fix the broken bird.

Years passed, and one day, the emperor fell ill. Everyone felt sorry for the emperor, as they thought he would die.

37

All on his own, the emperor stayed in bed with the broken nightingale next to him.

He thought about his past.

He felt so ill that he thought he was going to die.

"How I would love to listen to the song of a nightingale," he said.

Suddenly, there was a beautiful sound. There, in a tree outside the emperor's window, was the real nightingale!

Some people had told the little bird that the emperor was ill and going to die. So, she had come back to sing for him one more time.

All at once, the emperor felt much
better. He got out of bed and went
to the window.

"I'm sorry that I told you to go away," he said to the nightingale. "Please will you stay with me in the palace?"

The nightingale shook her head.
"My song sounds best in the forest,"
she said. "But I will come to this tree
every day and sing for you."

Everyone was astonished to see that the emperor was better. And it was all because of the little brown nightingale.

How much do you remember about the story of *The Emperor and the Nightingale*? Answer these questions and find out!

- What is the emperor's palace made of?

- Who does the emperor ask to find the nightingale for him?

- Who takes the lord to the forest?

- What is inside the box that is sent to the emperor?

- How much time passes before the clockwork nightingale breaks?

- Why won't the real nightingale stay in the palace when she comes back to sing for the emperor?